MR. JOSEPH

A Crow: Named PEDRO?

To order additional copies of this book, contact:
Xlibris
1-888-795-4274
www.Xlibris.com
Orders@Xlibris.com

A Crow:
Named Pedro?

Mr. Joseph

I want to thank my mother and father and then my stepmother, Betsy.

This was my first real rough draft of the story.

This is in dedication to Lyneah Rean Marie Matone
and a father's dream to my father, Mike.

They call him Pedro. He is a crow, but that is another story. Pedro tells his children the story about the flea and the fox.

There once was a fox named Tee, who just couldn't seem to ever be free. It was just one little flea.

He scratched from dusk till dawn with no sleep. In the morning, he rolled frantically in the dirt, praying for that one flea to depart. It couldn't hurt.

He rolled and rolled, shook and shivered. It seemed like that old flea gave him goose bumps, you see.

At times, the flea tickled his skin and sometimes got in a spot that made the old fox laugh, and he couldn't seem to stop. He laughed so hard it made him cry. At other times, he wanted to die just to be free of that little old flea.

He sat and wondered, *What can I do?* He tried to scratch and lick to no avail. The same old flea was still there.

He came up with a plan to trick the flea. He would go for a swim, with a stick in his mouth. Submerging his whole body, even his tail, he spent hours in the water, so cold and clear, with just his nose above and with that stick at bay for that flea to entail. He waited with not a peep or a movement at all. It was just a matter of time for that flea to be gone.

Well, he could feel that flea heading from far below, from his tail to his stomach, and then far above. From the top of his back to the tip of his nose, that flea was departing once and for all from the end of that stick to the outreach of the twig. He could see that old flea now far above. As soon as he felt it was time to let go, the flea was in the current on that twig, sailing on his own.

"Goodbye, goodbye," uttered Tee. You see, even a fox is smarter than a flea.

Well, that old fox felt so free. He shared that story with your daddy, which is me. For if you ever see a fox in a river with a stick in his mouth, he's not playing fetch but he, too, figured it out. This shows the end justifies the means. The fox will always be smarter than any old flea–unless you are that flea just wanting to be set free. After you've had all that fun and it's bedtime, you see. Good night and sleep well, my children.

The Arizona Crow

MY NAME IS Oscar. I am a wildcat. I live in the desert of Arizona. My family has lived here since the dawn of warm-blooded felines. Why, I am told that my family goes back to the age of the dinosaurs. Boys and girls, I am going to tell you a story about the Arizona crow. Why, he has been here as long as my family can remember, even longer. Even one Native American tribe named themselves after the crow. Settlers moved out here later.

Now this story was told by my great-grandpappy, Max. The crow only ate grain and vegetables at first. Some of his friends were Sammy Side Winder, Willy Bill Coyote, Lady Hawk, and Tommy the Rattlesnake. Well, that old crow was named Pedro. That's where the story begins.

Pedro supposedly moved one year looking for a home. Some people say he came from Mexico. Others say he was from the East Coast. He never really did have an accent. We just called him Pedro.

First, Pedro thought he'd live in the valley. He slept the first night on the ground. He didn't know much about the area but, he learned real fast. Why, between the coyotes, the sidewinders, and the rattlesnakes, I'd say he would be a belly full by the morning. That is not to exclude the wildcat family, mine. Anyway, he survived that night. The only problem in the desert was that no one could agree on anything. If it wasn't for the commotion of all those animals arguing over who was going to eat Pedro, I think Pedro would have been done for.

Well, this commotion woke Pedro up, startled. He flew high and fast. Finally, he found a hole in a cactus to stay in. This time of year, we get a lot of rain. It started to rain that night, and it rained and rained and rained. Pedro had just fallen asleep, listening to that sweet, soft pitter-patter sound of water hitting the desert's rock-hard, dry ground. Let me tell you what happens when it rains in the desert. See, rock-hard, dry ground doesn't absorb water. You know what that means, boys and girls? You're right! The water off those mountains is going to come tumbling down, and that's what it did. It's the fastest, meanest *roar of thunder* you would ever hear in your life. That water cuts a gorge ten feet deep and thirty feet wide, taking anything in its path with it. This time, Pedro heard that *roar* for the first time, but it was too late. Startled and scared, Pedro froze. That old cactus was first thrown forty feet straight up into the air, roots and all. Pedro held on for dear life. Well, within minutes, he was topside and probably going fifty miles per hour on top of that wave of water across the desert. He probably traveled one hundred miles that night before he came to a stop. That's when he met my grandpappy, my great-grandpappy at that. That's how my great-grandpappy first met Mr. Crow. Mr. Crow was beginning to become desert smart. He stayed a safe distance from my great-grandpappy, Mr. Max Wild Cat.

Well, Mr. Crow and Max talked for hours, even days. They had a lot of stories to tell each other, Max and that crow. Mr. Crow heard about the desert council made up of Mr. Owl, Sammy Side Winder, Willy Bill Coyote, Lady Hawk, Tommy Rattlesnake, and Buzzard. Pedro sat in on a desert council meeting. He didn't stay long though. He remembered the first night he stayed in the desert, and that desert council was the same bunch that woke him because they were arguing over who was going to get to eat him. Poor old Mr. Crow! He figured that they couldn't make a decision on that. In fact, they could not make a decision on much of anything else. The highest on the council was Lady Hawk. She basically had the final say over the council during the day. When she was asleep at night, Mr. Owl, the wise old owl, took control as second in command over the council; but he was too busy trying to think of a way to win Mr. Crow (Pedro) as a meal for himself. The noise was so loud it was even louder than coyote laughter at the moon. Why, I think it could have awakened those resting Native American spirits who had laid to rest for many, many moons in those mountains.

At first, no one thought much about Mr. Crow living with them. Mr. Crow was still looking for a place to call home and live. He flew up into those mountains for safety each and every night. Shortly afterward, some of the Indian tribes went to war. It seemed like Mr. Crow had been taking some of those Indians' belongings. At first, the Indians blamed one another. It didn't take long though before everyone knew it was Mr. Crow–Pedro to be exact.

Why, I remember settlers moved in with their house of logs—something you don't see out this way. They brought items that glittered and shined. Some you could even see your reflection in. Mr. Crow wandered into one of those cabins one day, knocked over a jar of white powder (flour), and made three or four trips out with what I believe they call jewelry. He collected bottle caps, marbles, rings, necklaces, and other various items that included a sewing thimble. Those settlers didn't really ever figure out the truth about Mr. Crow, even still today. Well, the Indians saw Mr. Crow that day. They tell the story about the great white ghost bird even today, but my family and I knew it was Mr. Crow—Pedro to be exact. The settlers didn't care much for Mr. Crow being in their gardens. They set up stakes that looked like people, even named them after Mr. Crow. They called them scarecrows. Some Indian drawings show the same concept without the name, a spirit watching over the corn crop, scaring the birds away.

Well, Mr. Crow met Mrs. Crow. They had a big wedding in the presence of the desert council. Lady Hawk performed the actual ceremony. It wasn't but two changing of seasons before there were three new arrivals into the crow family, each attaining the same principle of collecting valuable and nonvaluable items to hoard and maintain for their own self-gratification. If you ever get a chance to follow Mr. Crow before nightfall up into those mountains in Arizona, you might become the wealthiest person you could ever imagine, for what all Mr. Crow has acquired is hidden in those mountains for centuries.

I am going to tell you another story about how Mr. Crow deceived Lady Hawk and her clan. And if you are very patient and you watch Mr. Crow, you can even see him still taunting Lady Hawk and her clan about the incident today. Hawks do eat crows, but Lady Hawk passed a law for her clan not to play with Mr. Crow, for it is not right to ever play with your food before eating it.

One day, Lady Hawk was out at dusk. She just caught a mouse and was about to eat it when Mr. Crow showed up. Seems like Mr. Crow wasn't eating much with the Indians and settlers, placing figures that look like people in their field in which they named after, "the Scare Crow." Mr. Crow showed up gasping for breath and said that the council needed to meet and needed Lady Hawk's final decision on a matter right away. Lady Hawk knew she could not fly fast enough to carry her food with her. She figured it would be OK with Mr. Crow since he was a vegetarian. She knew the great desert buzzard would take her meal if she left it there unattended for more than half an hour. Since it was not after dusk yet, she still had rights over Mr. Owl in decisions. She had great pride in having this authority over the council, and that pride was probably what cost her that meal.

When she reached the council area, she found no one there. She flew reluctantly back to where she had left Mr. Crow with her enormous mouse. Seems like Mr. Crow had been planning this victory all along and must have been close by, watching her every move, watching her like a hawk. He planned an approach—a clever scheme to take advantage of the situation using all his poise and wits to accomplish the task, attain the prey without a fight or struggle, and return into the mountains shortly after dusk to feed his family. Even today, you will see Mr. Crow at the scene of a fresh dead animal, eating a rabbit, deer, goat, lamb, and even a coyote. This did not only change the council's relationship with Mr. Crow and he never joined the council. The reason why he never joined the council is because the same animals on the council were the same animals that could not make a decision on who was going to take him home and devour him. This also changed his eating habits and made him become a predator bird—a bird of prey without the hunting aspect—bringing him closer to the vulture. The crow had found that fresh dead animals are preferred, bringing him even closer to the hawk and the eagle. Pedro told Max this story about the hawk and asked that it be passed down through his family that crows need to be looked up to. They survive and strive where other birds have failed.

Printed in the United States
By Bookmasters